A. FRANK SMITH, JR. LIBRARY CENTER
Southwestern University
Georgetown, Texas 78626

DATE DUE

OCT 0 1 2000			
OCT 2 2 2000			

Demco No. 62-0549

WITHDRAWN

ELIZABETH SPURR

Lupe & Me

ILLUSTRATED BY

Enrique O. Sanchez

GULLIVER BOOKS

HARCOURT BRACE & COMPANY

San Diego   New York   London

Text copyright © 1995 by Elizabeth Spurr
Illustrations copyright © 1995 by Enrique O. Sanchez

All rights reserved. No part of this publication may be reproduced or transmitted in any form
or by any means, electronic or mechanical, including photocopy, recording, or any
information storage and retrieval system, without permission in writing from the publisher.

Requests for permission to make copies of any part of the work should be mailed to:
Permissions Department, Harcourt Brace & Company, 6277 Sea Harbor Drive,
Orlando, Florida 32887–6777.

Gulliver Books is a registered trademark of Harcourt Brace & Company.

Library of Congress Cataloging-in-Publication Data
Spurr, Elizabeth.
Lupe & me/written by Elizabeth Spurr; illustrated by Enrique O. Sanchez. — 1st ed.
p.   cm.
"Gulliver books."
Summary: Seven-year-old Susan forms a special friendship with her family's young
housekeeper, Lupe, who introduces her to Mexican customs and the Spanish language.
ISBN 0-15-200522-6
1. Mexicans — United States — Juvenile fiction. [1. Mexicans — United States — Fiction.
2. Household employees — Fiction. 3. Aliens, Illegal — Fiction.] I. Sanchez, Enrique O., ill.
II. Title.
PZ7.S7695Lu   1995
[Fic] — dc20   91-35824

Printed in Singapore

First edition
A B C D E

The paintings in this book were done in acrylics on canvas.
The display type was set in Celestia Italic.
The text type was set in Stempel Garamond by Thompson Type, San Diego, California.
Color separations were made by Bright Arts, Ltd., Singapore.
Printed and bound by Tien Wah Press, Singapore
This book was printed with soya-based inks on Leykam recycled paper, which contains more
than 20 percent postconsumer waste and has a total recycled content of at least 50 percent.
Production supervision by Warren Wallerstein and David Hough
Designed by Lori J. McThomas

CF
p95l

For Susan — and for Luz

— E. S.

For Siena

— E. O. S.

Contents

CHAPTER ONE

Lupe Comes to Our House

My father is gone. My mother works. Our house gets very messy. Or it used to, until Lupe came along.

Lupe was sent by the employment agency. She wore a pink ruffled dress and red tennis shoes and carried a brown paper shopping bag of clothes. She came one evening with a fat lady, who spoke in Spanish to Lupe and in English to my mother.

"Muy sucia," the lady said to Lupe. And to my mother, "Your house is very dirty."

She gave my mother a small Spanish/English dictionary. Then she winked good-bye to Lupe and left. Lupe stared at the mess. She looked scared.

My mother led Lupe to our guest room. Lupe's eyes grew big. She grinned and said, "¡Televisión!"

Lupe ran her fingers over the yellow daisy bedspread. She sat on the mattress and bounced a little. She took off her shoes and stretched out against the pillows. Then she yawned and said, "Estoy cansada."

My mother looked in her dictionary. "Come on, Susan," she said. "Lupe is tired."

I said, "Good night, Lupe."

She said, "Buenas noches, Susana."

Susana. That sounded much prettier than just plain Susie or Sue.

CHAPTER TWO

New Friends

The next day Lupe was dressed in jeans and a sweatshirt that read *Go Broncos!* The Broncos played football at the high school. My mother said Lupe was taking classes there at night.

Lupe always sang while she worked. She loved all our appliances — the dishwasher, the washer and dryer, the attachments for the vacuum cleaner. She worked hard, scrubbing and polishing, dusting and sweeping, and carrying out mountains of trash.

Until, finally, our home sparkled like her eyes when she said, *"¡Ah, bueno! Muy limpia."*

At first Lupe and I could not talk to each other. But our smiles could. So could our hands. I pointed to myself and held up seven fingers. Lupe said, *"¡Ah! Siete años."* I said, "I'm seven, almost eight."

Lupe held up ten plus six and said, *"Diez y seis."*

We taught each other words and giggled. We drew pictures in the air and giggled some more.

She pointed to my nose. *"La nariz."* Then to my mouth. *"La boca."*

She pointed to my eyes. *"Los ojos."* She held up two fingers. *"Dos ojos."*

I sat down on my bed. She said, *"La cama."*

She pointed again to my eyes. *"¿Los osos?"* I said.

Lupe giggled and giggled. *"¡No! ¡No!"* She pointed to the teddy bears on my bed. *"Los osos,"* she said.

I laughed, too. "Oh, I see. *Los osos* have *dos ojos.*"

"¡Sí! ¡Sí!" She smiled.

One of the bear's button eyes was hanging by a

thread. Lupe got her sewing kit and fixed it. When she had finished, I thanked her, *"Gracias."*

Lupe grinned and pointed to herself and then to me. *"Amigas,"* she said. *"Dos amigas."* I knew she meant we were friends.

Every morning I looked forward to seeing Lupe at breakfast. I would say *"Buenos días,"* and she would answer "Good morning, Susana," with long O's and rippling R's.

For breakfast Lupe beat eggs and poured them into the frying pan. They sizzled like a thin pancake. When the pancake was done, she spread it with jelly and rolled it up. When I ate it, the jelly dripped down my chin. Lupe's *huevos* were much more fun than boring scrambled eggs.

"¿Jugo de naranja?" she would ask as she poured the orange juice. She made all her J's sound like H's and laughed when I didn't.

She even taught my dog, Jason, to understand Spanish. She would hold up a bone and say, *"¡Venga, perro!"* And, believe it or not, the dog came.

Lupe loved to wash my hair and brush it dry in the sun. She taught me how to twist it into a long braid like hers. *"Ah, muy bonita,"* she would say when we were finished. That meant I looked pretty. My mother said that blond hair, *pelo rubio,* is rare in Mexico.

I learned many new things from Lupe. She taught me how to shine our copper pots with limes, how to clean windows with old newspapers, and how to make tea out of orange blossoms. She showed me how to pat flour and water into a ball and roll it into *tortillas,* which she baked on a griddle. We ate them with *salsa* made from green *tomatillos,* onions, and green chiles.

We wove hats from palm leaves, and we crocheted pot holders. We sewed the pot holders together to make a bedspread, but we didn't have enough so we made a shawl. Some days we made roses out of colored tissue paper or played a game, catching a ball in a cup. Whatever we did, Lupe made it fun.

Now that I didn't have to go to the sitter after

school, I could ask girls from my class to come home with me. In the clean, shiny kitchen, we ate Lupe's hot buttered *tortillas,* wove hats, and made paper roses.

Lupe wanted to become a singer. She played her *tía*'s guitar and taught us Spanish songs like *"La Golondrina."* Sometimes we clapped and danced to the music.

Every afternoon seemed like a party. I had many new friends. But none like Lupe.

CHAPTER THREE

Lupe's Family

On weekends Lupe stayed with her *tía* and her cousins. My mother and I drove her to her aunt's home every Friday night.

The house was old but had fresh white paint and a covered front porch trimmed with wood curlicues. The roof was strung with Christmas lights all year round, and the garden was filled with bright flowers.

In the garden was a small statue of a woman dressed in a blue-and-gold gown. *"La Virgen de*

Guadalupe," said Lupe. She pointed to herself. "*Mi patrona. ¿Entiendes?*"

"I see," I said. "*Lupe* is short for *Guadalupe*."

"*Sí*," she said.

Every week when we dropped Lupe off, her *tía* opened the screen door and put out her arms. Lupe's cousins tugged at her skirt as if she had been gone for a year. The radio played Mexican music, and the air was full of cooking smells. Sometimes I wished Mom and I could stay.

Each Monday morning, when Lupe returned, she would look around the kitchen, scowl, and say "*Muy sucia.*" Then she would hand me the dish towel and a mop. I'd laugh. She knew I had to leave for school.

One day I found out Lupe wasn't joking. She had let my mess wait. When I came home, she handed me the broom and turned on her *televisión.* All of us, even Jason, were more careful after that.

Often we went together to the post office, where Lupe would get a money order to send to her family in Guadalajara. She drew me a picture of the clay

tiles they would buy to put over the dirt floor of their home and the glass panes they would put in the windows. She showed me a photograph of her mother, three brothers, and two little sisters. She looked sad and put her hand over her heart.

CHAPTER FOUR

Christmastime

Lupe loved Christmastime. To her it was *La Navidad*. From rags and bottles and flour-and-water paste, she made a Nativity scene — Mary, Joseph, three wise men, and an angel. Then she made a crib out of Popsicle sticks. It was empty.

"But Lupe," I asked, "where's the baby?"

She shook her head and pointed to the calendar. "No *bebé* yet."

To prepare for the Christmas *fiesta*, she fried little meat pies called *empanadas*, wrapped *tamales*

A. FRANK SMITH, JR. LIBRARY CENTER
Southwestern University
Georgetown, Texas 78626

in corn husks, and made soups she called *sopas.* They tingled my nose with their warm, spicy smells. While she worked, Lupe softly hummed "Silent Night," which she called *"Noche de Paz."*

We made small, round white cookies from powdered sugar and butter, then pressed a nut in the middle of each one. From her aunt's house Lupe brought me a *piñata,* a hollow papier-mâché horse covered with red and white shredded tissue. She made me hide my eyes while she filled it; then we hung it up high.

On Christmas Eve our tree was lit and the fireplace was blazing. Lupe went to her room and brought out a tiny doll she had made from a stocking. With a solemn face she placed it in the crib and lit a candle. Then she smiled and said, *"Feliz Navidad."* I smiled back and said, "Merry Christmas."

She handed me a stick of firewood and motioned for me to break the *piñata.* I looked at my mother. She nodded. Then Lupe blindfolded me with a napkin.

I swung at the *piñata,* but not very hard. I did

not want to ruin the beautiful horse. I swung again, and it fell to the floor without breaking. It was filled with wrapped candies and little bags of the cookies we had made. Some of the cookies spilled out of the bags. Jason was there in a flash.

"No, Jason!" I yelled. But he had already gulped down several.

Lupe laughed and hugged him. "Merry Christmas, doggy."

CHAPTER FIVE

A Birthday Surprise

On the morning of my birthday party, Lupe shut herself in the kitchen. She told me not to come in because she was making a *sorpresa*, a surprise.

When my friends arrived, she was still working. They brought presents wrapped in fancy paper and ribbon. In the dining room Lupe had hung another *piñata*. This time it was shaped like a rooster and filled with wrapped candies, gumballs, and tiny toys, one for each guest.

After we had broken the *piñata* and I had

opened all my gifts, Lupe came out of the kitchen. She carried a cake that had no frosting and only one candle. "A *torta*." She smiled proudly and said, "*Feliz cumpleaños.*" I knew that meant "Happy birthday."

"*¡Muchas gracias!* Oh, Lupe, thank you so much!" I made a wish, blew out the candle, and cut the cake. It was made of honey and nuts. My friends looked at each other. One of them said, "Where are the pink sugar roses?" Lupe was back in the kitchen. I hoped she did not hear.

Lupe came back with another dessert, a plate of little white mounds covered with brown syrup. "This is *flan*," she told us. "Very special for your *fiesta*."

My friends whispered and giggled. One of them said, "*Ewww,* custard!"

They did not eat much. But I did. The *flan* tasted like ice cream, but it wasn't cold.

When my friends left, I went to the kitchen. Lupe was scraping the desserts into the sink. She looked very sad. "They did not like my *sorpresa*."

"What do we care?" I said. "All the more for us!"

Lupe laughed and dished out two plates of *flan* and *torta*. We had another birthday party at the kitchen table.

When the dishes were done, Lupe went to her room and brought me a ball of purple tissue paper. Inside was a small painted box containing eight tiny dolls. They were made of wire and thread and were smaller than my thumb.

"Oh, Lupe! This is the best gift of all."

"Por los problemas," said Lupe. I knew what she meant. If you have a problem, you put it in the box and let the little people worry for you.

It seemed like a good idea.

CHAPTER SIX

Problemas

Sometimes Lupe and I took walks downtown. She loved to look in the shop windows at pretty clothes and shoes, and to point at fancy furniture and dishes. She laughed a lot and her eyes were bright. But every now and then she would look over her shoulder, as if she were frightened.

"What's the matter, Lupe?" I would ask.

She'd shake her head, whisper *"Nada,"* and gaze at the windows again.

But I could tell she was often worried about

something. I wondered if I should lend her my little box of dolls for her *problemas*.

One day Jason dug under the fence and disappeared. I told the worry people, and in less than an hour a man in uniform brought him back. When Lupe saw the man's badge, she hid in her room. Later she whispered, "*¿Policía?*" I laughed and said, "Dogcatcher."

Not long after that Lupe got a phone call. She spoke very fast and waved her hands. Her black eyes flashed.

After she put down the phone, she went to her room and shut the door. She did not wish me *buenas noches*. She did not turn on her TV. And I could hear her crying in the night.

CHAPTER SEVEN

Lupe Disappears

The next morning the kitchen was quiet. The coffeepot was cold. Jason's bowl was empty. Where was Lupe?

I knocked on her door. There was no answer. I peeked in. Her bed was made. I went to the closet. The pink ruffled dress, red tennis shoes, and brown shopping bag were gone.

My mother called the employment agency. The number had been disconnected. We called Lupe's *tía*. Her number was disconnected, too.

The next day my mother and I drove to the white house. It was empty. There was a FOR RENT sign on the picket fence. The flowers in the garden were drooping. And there was no statue of *La Virgen*.

For days I sat by the window with my box of worry people. Where was Lupe? I shut my problem in the box, but the worries leaked out. No more walks. No more songs. No more games or giggles. And worst of all, I had to go back to the sitter.

Oh, Lupe, why did you leave?

At last the postman brought a letter. The envelope was stamped Guadalajara! I ran to my mother and showed her. She brought out the Spanish/English dictionary.

The letter was written in pencil on blue-lined paper, and it was very short. It said that Lupe, her aunt, and cousins had left because they were worried about *la migra*. She sent her love and signed, *"Muchas gracias,* Lupe." The P.S. said to give Jason a cookie.

"La migra," said my mother. "I had no idea! So that's why the agency went out of business."

A. FRANK SMITH, JR. LIBRARY CENTER
Southwestern University
Georgetown, Texas 78626

"*¿La migra?*" I pictured a bogeyman. No wonder Lupe had looked frightened.

"Lupe must have come here illegally." My mother explained that *la migra* meant the immigration police. Lupe could not return to this country until she had a green card.

CHAPTER EIGHT

Waiting

I talked to the worry people; then I had an idea. In the gift shop I found a greeting card. It was green. I sent the card to Lupe.

I told my mother about the card. She smiled, but her eyes were sad. "Lupe will be happy to hear from you," she said. "But the green card she needs comes from the INS, the immigration service. It gives people from other countries permission to live and work in the United States."

"Can't we get her one?" I asked.

She shook her head. "I'm not sure."

"Oh, please, please," I said. "We have to."

"We'll see," said my mother. "We'll see what we can do." She put her arm around me. "You know, I miss Lupe, too."

That was in September, just before school started. Now it's almost Christmas again. Every day from my bedroom window, Jason and I and the worry people watch for her: pink ruffled dress, red tennis shoes, brown shopping bag — and a green card.

But, meanwhile, I dust and wash dishes and tidy up to keep our house *muy limpia* for Lupe's return.

Glossary

amigas	friends
bebé	baby
la boca	the mouth
buenos días	good morning
buenas noches	good night
bueno	good
la cama	the bed
diez y seis	sixteen
dos amigas	two friends
dos ojos	two eyes
empanada	a turnover with a sweet or savory filling
¿Entiendes?	Do you understand?
estoy cansada	I am tired
Feliz cumpleaños	Happy birthday
Feliz Navidad	Merry Christmas
fiesta	party
flan	a custard dessert, often topped with caramel sauce

gracias	thank you
huevos	eggs
¿Jugo de naranja?	(Would you like some) orange juice?
"La Golondrina"	"The Swallow," a traditional song
la migra	the immigration police
mi patrona	my patron saint
muchas gracias	thank you very much
muy bonita	very pretty
muy limpia	very clean
muy sucia	very dirty
nada	nothing
la nariz	the nose
La Navidad	Christmas
"Noche de Paz"	"Silent Night"
los ojos	the eyes
los osos	the bears
pelo rubio	blond hair
piñata	a hollow papier-mâché figurine decorated with shredded tissue paper and filled with goodies

policía	police
por los problemas	for your problems
problemas	problems
salsa	a sauce made with tomatoes, onions, and green chiles
sí	yes
siete años	seven years
sopas	soups
sorpresa	surprise
tamale	ground meat rolled in cornmeal dough, wrapped in corn husks, and steamed
televisión	television
tía	aunt
tomatillo	fruit resembling a small tomato
torta	cake
tortilla	flat round cake of unleavened cornmeal or wheat flour
¡Venga, perro!	Come, dog!
La Virgen de Guadalupe	the Virgin of Guadalupe, an important religious symbol